Great Jobs in Business

Craig E. Blohm

San Diego, CA

About the Author
Craig E. Blohm has written numerous books and magazine articles for young readers. He and his wife, Desiree, reside in Tinley Park, Illinois.

© 2019 ReferencePoint Press, Inc.
Printed in the United States

For more information, contact:
ReferencePoint Press, Inc.
PO Box 27779
San Diego, CA 92198
www.ReferencePointPress.com

ALL RIGHTS RESERVED.
No part of this work covered by the copyright hereon may be reproduced or used in any form or by any means—graphic, electronic, or mechanical, including photocopying, recording, taping, web distribution, or information storage retrieval systems—without the written permission of the publisher.

Picture Credits:

Cover: EmirMemedovski/iStockphoto.com
 6: Maury Aaseng
12: fizkes/iStockphoto.com
19: Monkey Business images/Shutterstock.com
30: Monkey Business images/Shutterstock.com

LIBRARY OF CONGRESS CATALOGING-IN-PUBLICATION DATA

Names: Blohm, Craig E., 1948– author.
Title: Great Jobs in Business/by Craig E. Blohm.
Description: San Diego, CA: ReferencePoint Press, Inc., [2019] | Series: Great Jobs | Includes bibliographical references and index.
Identifiers: LCCN 2018033106 (print) | LCCN 2018035024 (ebook) | ISBN 9781682825181 (eBook) | ISBN 9781682825174 (hardback)
Subjects: LCSH: Business—Vocational guidance—Juvenile literature. | Occupations—Juvenile literature.
Classification: LCC HF5381.2 (ebook) | LCC HF5381.2 .B56 2019 (print) | DDC 331.702—dc23
LC record available at https://lccn.loc.gov/2018033106

Contents

Introduction: Business in the New Millennium	4
Market Research Analyst	8
Training and Development Specialist	17
Small Business Owner	26
Financial Analyst	34
Public Relations Specialist	42
Sales Engineer	50
Franchise Owner	58
Accountant and Auditor	66
Interview with a Public Relations Specialist	74
Other Jobs in Business	77
Index	78

Introduction

Business in the New Millennium

In the twenty-first century, business in America is booming. Stimulated by such factors as growing international trade, changes in society's demographics, and rapid advances in technology, business drives the country's place in the global economy. At its most basic, business can be defined as the creating and selling of a product or service. But there is more to business than is embodied in that simple definition. Successful businesses rely on people with diverse skills and personalities working together to accomplish a company's goals. Accountants and financial analysts, for example, are essential in keeping a business profitable. Marketing analysts determine what the consumer wants and how the company can fulfill those desires. Advertising specialists inform the public about a company's products or services. Sales executives set sales goals and encourage their sales teams to meet those goals. Training specialists help enhance employee skills and knowledge. And managers keep a business's day-to-day operations running smoothly and efficiently.

A business can be as large as General Motors, as small as a one-person online shop, or just about anything in between. A family-owned mom-and-pop store selling goods from clothing to hardware can offer a rewarding career. Working in a fast-paced, multinational firm can bring big financial rewards as well as the feeling of being part of a world-changing industry. It is between these two extremes where thousands of business jobs exist in almost any field imaginable. These jobs may involve working alone or with others as a part of a team, working in an office or traveling the world, crunching numbers, or creating television commercials. In short, there is a business job that can fit almost anyone's skills and personality.

Education for Business

The foundation of a business is its dedicated and knowledgeable employees. A college degree in business can give a student the education required to pursue a successful business career. Of the more than 1.9 million bachelor's degrees awarded in 2016, according to the *Digest of Education Statistics*, a publication of the National Center for Education Statistics, 371,694 were in the field of business, surpassing all other majors. At the master's degree level, business topped all other fields, conferring 185,000 degrees.

College students who major in business generally have a choice of numerous fields of study. As Laura Tucker, a former staff writer for TopUniversities.com, explains,

> If you're someone who enjoys the professionalism and high-powered nature of big business, then you're likely to be considering a business degree as a stepping stone to a high-status, high-salary career. In today's world, corporate business careers are available in pretty much every sector you can think of; all industries need strong leaders, managers, financial advisors and market-savvy decision-makers. For many business graduates, however, the traditional pathways still hold a strong appeal—including careers in the banking and financial sectors, consultancy, human resources and marketing roles.

University business programs usually offer numerous options in a wide variety of disciplines: accounting, economics, entrepreneurship, finance, general management, international business, marketing, management information systems, organizational behavior, public policy, and operations research. According to Tucker, a business degree "can open you up to many entry-level roles

Great Jobs in Business

Occupation	Minimum Educational Requirement	2017 Median Pay
Accountant and auditor	Bachelor's degree	$69,350
Bookkeeper, accountant, auditing clerk	Some college, no degree	$39,240
Cashier	No formal education credential	$21,030
Customer service representative	High school diploma or equivalent	$32,890
Food service manager	High school diploma or equivalent	$52,030
Human resources specialist	Bachelor's degree	$60,350
Insurance underwriter	Bachelor's degree	$69,760
Loan officer	Bachelor's degree	$64,660
Market research analyst	Bachelor's degree	$63,230
Real estate broker and sales agent	High school diploma or equivalent	$47,880
Software developer	Bachelor's degree	$103,560
Travel agent	High school diploma or equivalent	$36,990

Source: Bureau of Labor Statistics, *Occupational Outlook Handbook*, 2018. www.bls.gov.

upon graduation, while still allowing those who wish to specialize further the chance to improve their return on investment with a graduate degree." Not all business programs necessarily lead to a place in the corporate world. "If a straightforward corporate career is failing to get you excited," Tucker says, "then a business program can also give you the skills to create your own business, or to take on business and management roles within more creative industries, be that fashion, media, or even the charity sector."

A Changing Business Environment

In the first decades of the twenty-first century, America experienced numerous changes, from an increasingly aging population to uncertainty in its international alliances. Business is not immune to this environment of change; it reacts, for better or worse, to changes in society and the world. According to the Business Insider website, the best business jobs for the future include financial managers, manufacturing sales representatives, personal financial advisers, and office supervisors.

But change can also hasten the demise of certain job categories. Many jobs that were important in past decades have become obsolete as technology has taken over labor that once only humans could perform. The US Bureau of Labor Statistics lists several business-oriented jobs that are predicted to decline over the next decade, including word processors and typists, computer operators, insurance claims adjusters, and data entry keyers.

The person who holds a degree in one of the many business disciplines and has a positive work ethic can prosper despite this environment of change. Business skills, such as accounting, managing, and marketing, are usually transferrable among different industries. This allows business majors to seek new opportunities or better position themselves for the possibility of advancement.

The jobs described in this book are all essential in helping to keep American business the most efficient and profitable in the world. In every area of the US economy—retail, finance, health care, manufacturing, education, or technology—there will always be a need for people with a solid interest in business and the drive to make their dreams succeed.

Market Research Analyst

At a Glance

Market Research Analyst

Minimum Educational Requirements
Bachelor's degree

Personal Qualities
Analytical skills; attention to detail; proficiency in written and interpersonal communication; creativity

Certification and Licensing
Not required but can enhance professional credibility

Working Conditions
Office environment

Salary Range
About $34,510 to $122,770 per year in 2016

Number of Jobs
595,400 in 2016

Future Job Outlook
Projected increase of 23 percent through 2026, which is much faster than average

What Does a Market Research Analyst Do?

The goal of any business, whether it manufactures a product or provides a service, is to sell its goods or services to customers. To be successful, a company's products and services must meet the needs of the people it wishes to reach. Determining who those people are and what products they are likely to be interested in is the job of a market research analyst.

Market research analysts gather information on consumer preferences and behavior, analyze the current conditions of the marketplace, and determine what a company's competitors are doing. They attempt to understand what kinds of products people want and how much they are likely to pay for them. If more people prefer, say, Ford automobiles over Chevrolets, the market research analyst conducts studies to determine why such a preference exists and how a loyal Ford owner might be persuaded to change to Chevrolet.

Statistics are the market research analyst's key to learning about the marketplace and its customers. Much of the statistical information reflects consumer shopping habits, brand preferences, and needs and desires. However, analysts will also examine an organization's advertising strategy to reveal which ads are most effective in selling a client's product and which media provide the best sales results. In addition, analysts keep tabs on their firm's competitors—including product prices, sales figures, and marketing strategies—to note trends and opportunities.

Market research analysts have many tools at their disposal to gather these statistics. Many of these tools are traditional methods that have been used for decades: focus groups, questionnaires, personal or telephone interviews, and public opinion polls. Field marketers go to public places such as shopping malls to gather research data in person by asking shoppers to take a brief survey about a product, service, or company. Telemarketers collect data by making random cold calls to people whose landline or cell phone number is listed in telephone directories and public records, or through social media or other sources on the Internet. The market research analyst uses this information to gauge public opinion and figure out how a company's products or services will perform in the marketplace.

In today's fast-changing marketplace, cutting-edge technology is also available for statistical research. Ted Donnelly, the managing director for the marketing research group Baltimore Research, tells *U.S. News & World Report*, "Our industry has changed so much in the last five years. We have so many new tools in the tool kit." For example, the Wi-Fi, Bluetooth, and GPS features of today's smartphones can be used to gather consumer data and indicate to analysts the most popular store locations or the effectiveness of a digital advertisement.

Once all the pertinent statistical information has been collected, the market research analyst uses sophisticated software to evaluate the data. While statistics may appear to be simply lists of numbers, the market research analyst not only interprets the raw data but must understand the human motivations and attitudes behind them. From this information, he or she develops market forecasts, recognizes likely openings for new products, and identifies potential new customers. Analysts then use these predictions to create marketing plans, advertising brochures, print ads, and media spots to expand the reach of their company's products or services.

The next step for the market research analyst is to determine the best way to present research results to clients in a meaningful and easy-to-understand way. This usually means a written report, but analysts may also make use of charts and graphs, PowerPoint presentations, videos, and other visual aids. Having a creative mind is helpful in this presentation phase. Researcher Matthew Harrison thought he had wowed an audience with a presentation only to be told later that his clients had been bored to tears. On research organization B2B International's website, Harrison says that market research is "all about storytelling." He clarifies, "Yes, our starting point is the systematic and objective collection of data, but there is only one thing that is going to make a set of research recommendations listened to, adhered to and returned to, and that is a convincing story well told."

The ability to determine what information to collect, to find the best methods of collection, to interpret the results, and to deliver those results in a creative way are the hallmarks of a successful market research analyst. It is a job that can influence both business practices and consumer behavior to keep America's economy strong.

How Do You Become a Market Research Analyst?

Education

Market research analysts usually have a bachelor's degree in market research or another business field, such as business administration, mathematics, statistics, or computer science. Classes in psychology, sociology, economics, English, and visual communication will provide useful skills for the various types of tasks a market research analyst must perform. Writing research papers and creating presentations with PowerPoint or similar software for class assignments provide a good basis for effective communication as a market research analyst. As competition for jobs is likely to increase in the future, job seekers with a master's degree will have an advantage in securing jobs with the highest pay.

Certification and Licensing

Although certification is not required to be a market research analyst, the Insights Association, the trade organization of the market research community, offers a professional researcher certificate (PRC). Having a PRC indicates a researcher's up-to-date understanding of ethical standards, research techniques, and knowledge of the market research field. Completion of twelve industry-related education hours and three years of relevant experience are required before taking the final certification exam.

The American Marketing Association also offers certification through its professional certified marketer program. Certification is available in digital marketing, content marketing, and marketing management.

Volunteer Work and Internships

Many market research companies provide internships for college juniors or seniors, or graduates interested in gaining experience in the field. Many internships are held over the summer months; some internships are paid, but others provide work experience but no compensation. Under supervision, interns perform day-to-day tasks such as helping to gather and interpret data, creating graphs and charts, assisting in developing marketing campaigns, and preparing reports for management.

Alyssa Dalrymple, a market research intern at Research and Marketing Strategies, is enthusiastic about her internship. "I love that I have the opportunity to work on a variety of tasks during any

A market research analyst presents data she has gathered on her company's consumer preferences and behavior. Presentations like this are a frequent part of the job.

given day," she writes on the company website. "What's more, I can actually see how what I do is directly used by the company. I've . . . worked with statistical software and the results from a survey and focus groups that will be developed into client reports. . . . It's exciting to see every aspect of a project come together to form meaningful information."

Skills and Personality

Successful market research analysts usually display proficiency in several areas. Most important are strong analytical skills, which involve the ability to understand statistical data and other raw information and turn them into meaningful insights for a client. To process data, knowledge of software such as Microsoft Excel, Google Analytics, and SPSS Statistics is an essential component of the market research analyst's job. "Someone who would enjoy this line of work," says Kate, a market research analyst, in a video on the OwlGuru website, "is someone who likes to be on the computer and do research. It's almost like a little bit of a puzzle, because you're putting the pieces together and finding out information." Good interpersonal communication skills are also necessary for working with clients and presenting research findings in an interesting and understandable way.

Several personality traits are desirable for a career in market research. According to marketing specialist Chris Martin, writing on the FlexMR website, "A key skill for any profession which involves social interaction is empathy—the ability to connect and bond with others is vital in market research. Participants have a range of personalities. Some will be willing and open to sharing their experiences immediately. But others will be naturally more reserved and require encouragement to engage with the research study."

Being detail oriented is another vital trait because market research analysts work daily with large quantities of comprehensive information. Being open-minded, flexible, methodical, and curious are also valuable qualities in market research. Participating in a team environment, having a natural affinity for mathematics, and possessing a creative mind that is always looking for new solutions to a client's needs are other helpful qualities of the successful market research analyst.

On the Job

Employers

According to the Bureau of Labor Statistics (BLS), in 2016 there were 595,400 people working as market research analysts in the United States. There is no typical employer, as market research is an important aspect of nearly all types of businesses, from major corporations and advertising agencies to small research firms that provide services for local clients. Although about 90 percent of market research analysts work in private industry, public entities such as government agencies, universities, hospitals, and libraries may also employ market researchers. For example, the US

Department of Energy uses analysts to research financial matters for its loan programs. Boston Children's Hospital conducts market analysis to help with strategic marketing and reinforce its reputation as a world-class hospital. Some market research firms offer a broad range of services for their clients, but others specialize in a single type of research in a specific area, such as education, agriculture, and health care.

Working Conditions

Most market research analysts work in an office environment, usually on a standard forty-hour-per-week schedule. Overtime may be required when tight deadlines must be met for a particular project. Occasionally a market research analyst may accompany interviewers or polltakers into the field to supervise their work. Most market research is performed on an individual basis, although the analyst may also work with a team on certain projects. There are also opportunities for market research analysts to work independently as freelancers, charging an hourly rate for their services.

Earnings

The BLS reports that the median annual salary for a market research analyst was $62,560. Compensation ranged from less than $34,510 for the lowest 10 percent to more than $122,770 for the highest 10 percent. Full-time market research analysts usually also receive company benefits, such as medical and dental insurance, paid vacations, sick leave, and contributions to retirement plans.

Opportunities for Advancement

Most market research analysts begin their careers as research assistants, performing such tasks as creating surveys and tabulating results. After gaining practical experience, the market research analyst will be given his or her own research project to conduct, individually or as part of a marketing team. From there, advancement will usually progress to assistant manager, research manager, and, in large firms, possibly to research executive or research department director. The path to the executive suite will often require changing employers, perhaps many times, throughout a person's career.

What Is the Future Outlook for Market Research Analysts?

The job outlook for market research analysts will grow much faster than average, according to the BLS, which projects a 23 percent increase through 2026. As online shopping continues to redefine the marketplace and traditional manufacturers and retailers experience intense competition for customers, market research will become even more important for the future of American business. College graduates with a broad knowledge of marketing, statistics, and research software will be in a good position to enter the market research field.

Find Out More

Advertising Research Foundation (ARF)
432 Park Ave. South
New York, NY 10016
website: www.thearf.org

The Advertising Research Foundation's mission is to further the scientific practice of advertising and marketing through research. It conducts annual conferences, provides networking via local ARF Councils, and promotes professional education through ARF Young Pros, a career development and leadership program.

American Association of Public Opinion Research (AAPOR)
One Parkview Plaza, Suite 800
Oakbrook Terrace, IL 60181
website: www.aapor.org

The American Association for Public Opinion Research is a professional organization dedicated to advancing the field of survey and opinion research. Student members of AAPOR can qualify for travel assistance to AAPOR's annual conference and are eligible to compete for prizes in student paper and poster competitions.

American Marketing Association (AMA)
130 E. Randolph St.
Chicago, IL 60601
website: www.ama.org

The American Marketing Association is the professional organization for people in marketing. The AMA Student Career Resources sponsors campus visits by representatives of marketing and other companies. The organization holds a collegiate career fair in conjunction with its annual International Collegiate Conference.

Insights Association
1156 Fifteenth St. NW, Suite 302
Washington, DC 20005
website: www.insightsassociation.org

A merger of two major market research groups, the Insights Association is the largest professional organization for market research analysts. It is an advocate for the industry, offers resources and networking for the marketing research and analytics community, and provides professional certification for market research analysts.

Training and Development Specialist

At a Glance

Training and Development Specialist

Minimum Educational Requirements
Bachelor's degree

Personal Qualities
Oral and written communication skills; leadership; creativity; attention to detail; ability to think under pressure

Certification and Licensing
Not required

Working Conditions
Office environment

Salary Range
About $33,150 to $102,340 per year in 2016

Number of Jobs
282,800 in 2016

Future Job Outlook
11 percent growth through 2026, which is faster than average

What Does a Training and Development Specialist Do?

When high school or college students graduate after four years of hard work, they have gained knowledge and skills that can pave the way to a rewarding career in their chosen field. But education does not stop after the diploma is hung on the wall. Every business has its own methods, operational procedures, and regulations that its employees must become familiar with to effectively support the company and its goals. Educating a company's workers is the job of the training and development specialist.

Training and development specialists design and conduct programs that help employees enhance knowledge of their position, improve their job skills, and guide them through advancement in the company. The specialist also trains employees in the latest company policies that may affect them, such as safety in the workplace, working with hazardous materials, or dealing with government regulations. The specialist's job encompasses developing programs for all levels of an organization, from the new hire to the experienced worker and from the middle manager to the top executive.

Training and development specialists analyze the training requirements of a business by conducting focus groups, interviewing employees, and consulting with management. After determining a company's training needs, the specialist produces educational programs that address those needs. There is a wide variety of materials and methods that can be employed in a training situation. The most basic type of training material is the printed word, which may be presented in the form of informational handouts, guideline sheets, or manuals. In addition, audiovisual material, such as videos and PowerPoint presentations, can make complicated information easy to understand. Training specialist Kim Wynans describes her job on the Virtual Inc. website:

> As a Training Specialist, I am responsible for planning the training class from start to finish, and my tasks can vary greatly. I work with both my client contact, events team and the class trainer to organize the training class. To do this, I need to combine the elements of an administrative wizard, a trouble-shooter, a problem-solver, a logistics queen and a customer service guru all into one job title—Training Specialist. Part of what I love about being a Training Specialist is that I often come up against challenges that are completely unexpected, so the solutions are equally surprising.

For new employees, the training and development specialist creates and administers orientation programs that help the newcomer understand how the company works and how his or her position integrates with the business's overall goals. Developing such a program may entail writing a new-employee handbook, preparing

A training and development specialist begins an orientation program for a newly hired employee. These specialists develop such programs to familiarize new employees with company priorities and procedures.

an audiovisual presentation, or creating a training course that a new employee can take using a computer or tablet. Such programs are vital to a company's success. "A thoughtful new employee orientation program can reduce turnover and save an organization thousands of dollars," says human resources expert Susan Heathfield on the Balance Careers website. "One reason people change jobs is because they never feel welcome or part of the organization they join." The training and development specialist is an important part of making sure that new hires turn into valuable employees.

Employees who have been with a business for years also benefit from the work of a training and development specialist. Companies are always seeking to improve their products or services for their customers. Changing a product line, adding new products, or adjusting a manufacturing method may require retraining workers. Rapidly evolving technology may also force changes in the workplace: if new machinery is installed or computer software upgrades are implemented, employees must be trained in new operational techniques.

The training and development specialist must be able to present information in many different ways. These can include seminars, group discussions, role-playing, lectures presented on video or in person, and one-on-one mentoring. Technology is becoming an increasingly important tool for training and development specialists. Virtual reality training programs, which feature three-dimensional environments and often include tactile interactive feedback, provide an immersive experience for trainees. One advantage of such programs is that they allow the trainee to experience working in hazardous situations without the danger of being in a dangerous real-life environment.

A training and development specialist must be able to evaluate the results of his or her training programs and modify them if necessary to produce maximum effectiveness. Training budgets need to be created and periodically reviewed to ensure economical operation of a company's training operation. Budget reports are prepared and given to management for approval. In a large organization, the training and development specialist will often supervise a team of instructors, assigning teaching duties, monitoring an instructor's performance, and suggesting areas for improvement.

According to a 2016 survey, as reported on the Access Perks website, 68 percent of employees said that training and development is the most important policy in the workplace, and 87 percent of millennials list professional development as very important. In addition, one of the top four reasons retail employees leave a position is due to the lack of training. These facts show that training and development specialists are a vital part of today's business environment.

How Do You Become a Training and Development Specialist?

Education

For an entry-level position as a training and development specialist, a bachelor's degree is required. This degree may be in any academic discipline, but preferred areas include training and development, instructional technology, human resources, and education. Degrees in business administration or one of the social sciences, such as psychology, sociology, or communication, may also be helpful in gaining a first job in training and development. As computer technology continues to play an ever-increasing role in business, candidates for a training and development specialist position may find a degree in information technology or computer science useful.

Certification and Licensing

Although certification is not required for the position of training and development specialist, several organizations offer opportunities to enhance an individual trainer's knowledge and skills through courses that lead to certificates. The Association for Talent Development offers a Certified Professional in Learning and Performance certificate, and the Institute for Performance and Learning offers the Certified Training and Development Professional certificate. Benefits of certification can include higher salaries and increased professional credibility. Certification might also make a trainer more attractive to potential employers.

Volunteer Work and Internships

Many human resources departments offer internships for training and development specialist positions. Interns will learn the basic day-to-day operations of the department and perform such tasks as assisting in analyzing the organization's training needs, monitoring training progress, proofreading or editing training materials, and making recommendations for improvements in training programs. Internships in training and development may be paid or unpaid, and they may be conducted full-time or during the summer.

Skills and Personality

A variety of skills are needed to be a successful training and development specialist. Foremost among these are oral and written communication skills: the ability to write a training program and then present it in a form that employees will understand

and remember. Leadership skills are also important, as training specialist Lisa Robles points out on the G.I. Jobs website. "To effectively provide training," Robles says, "leadership skills are imperative. There is a level of difficulty to engaging and changing someone's view on how they approach their work."

Technology skills are becoming increasingly important in training and development. Specialists must be familiar with classroom technology, online learning platforms, and management system software. As vital as technological knowledge has become, interpersonal skills are even more important. Training and development specialists must be able to identify the needs of their audience and create a training program that serves those needs; likewise, they also must be proficient in adjusting the message in response to audience reactions.

The field of training and development is so varied that many personality types can find success in the field. Sue Kaiden is the credentialing project manager for the Association for Talent Development's Certification Institute. She discusses training and development personality types on the organization's website:

> Because the field is so diverse, there truly are opportunities for every personality type. The key will be to make sure that your personality matches the type of training and corporate culture of the company for which you will be working. So, for example, if you enjoy technical subjects and structured environments, you might gravitate towards a larger company that needs technical trainers. On the other hand, if you love unstructured environments and can deal with uncertainty, you might enjoy a tech start-up.

Attention to detail and the ability to think under pressure are also valuable personality traits. And those with a creative personality who enjoy developing new training concepts and designing courses and other learning materials will do well as a training and development specialist.

On the Job

Employers

Training and development specialists are a valuable part of most industries. The Bureau of Labor Statistics (BLS) lists several of the largest employers of training and development specialists. These include professional, technical, and scientific services; health care and social assistance; finance and insurance; educational services; and administrative and support services. Training and development specialists may work in human resource departments under the supervision of a training and development director, or they may work as consultants for an independent training company.

Working Conditions

Training and development specialists generally work a standard forty-hour week in a comfortable office environment. Occasional overtime may be required. In a large corporation, travel from the company headquarters to branch offices or off-site training locations may also be required.

Earnings

According to the BLS, the median annual salary for a training and development specialist in 2016 was $59,020. The highest-paid specialists earned more than $102,340, and the lowest-paid ones earned less than $33,150. Median salaries ranged from $50,890 per year for training and development specialists in administrative and support services to $68,870 for those in professional, technical, and scientific services

Opportunities for Advancement

After several years of experience, a training and development specialist may advance to become a training supervisor, overseeing the work of a team of training specialists. With additional experience, and often after obtaining a master's degree in business, education, or communication, advancement to training and development manager or human resources manager is possible.

Specialists who have developed skills in social media, computer learning, visual communication, and other technological innovations in training methods will be particularly suited for advancement. For self-starters, another avenue for advancement may be to form an independent consulting company and develop a roster of clients.

What Is the Future Outlook for Training and Development Specialists?

The BLS projects jobs for training and development specialists to grow at a rate of 11 percent through 2026. This is faster than the average rate of growth for all occupations. As businesses grow and introduce new technology and operating procedures, the importance of expert training and development specialists will keep this career in demand for the foreseeable future.

Find Out More

American Management Association (AMA)
1601 Broadway
New York, NY 10019
website: www.amanet.org

The AMA offers educational programs, conferences, online training, and publications for professionals working in various aspects of human resources. The AMA offers specially selected programs to meet the needs of training and development professionals, including seminars on the latest training technologies, tips for in-house training procedures, and information on improving instructional design.

Association for Talent Development (ATD)
1640 King St.
Alexandria, VA 22314
website: www.td.org

The Association for Talent Development is a nonprofit organization dedicated to setting standards for the industrial training profession and furthering the professional's education and development. The ATD conducts research on workplace learning, holds an annual conference, and provides career services and certification for training and development specialists.

International Society for Performance Improvement (ISPI)
PO Box 13035
Silver Spring, MD 20910
website: www.ispi.org

The International Society for Performance Improvement is an international organization dedicated to improving workplace performance through instructional and noninstructional methods. The ISPI holds an annual conference and a monthly webinar, publishes a professional journal, and has an award of excellence program to showcase excellence in the field.

Society for Human Resource Management (SHRM)
1800 Duke St.
Alexandria, VA 22314
website: www.shrm.org

The world's largest professional human resources organization, the SHRM has members in more than 165 countries. Its stated mission is to serve the human resources community, providing education, thought leadership, certification, community, and advocacy to enhance the practice of human resource management and the effectiveness of human resource professionals in the organizations and communities they serve.

Small Business Owner

What Does a Small Business Owner Do?

When the word *business* is mentioned, many people may think first of big business—large corporations making everything from cars and computers to frozen food and ballpoint pens. But the surprising truth is that 99.9 percent of all firms in the United States are small businesses—and these businesses are driving the US economy.

According to the US Small Business Administration (SBA), a small business is an independent firm that employs fewer than five hundred people. In 2016 there were 29.6 million small businesses in the United States, compared to 19,000 big businesses. These small operations accounted for 63 percent of all new jobs between 2010 and 2016 and employed a total of 58 million workers. Most small businesses have fewer than one hundred employees; some, called nonemployer firms, are operated solely by the owner and employ no paid workers. Today small business en-

At a Glance

Small Business Owner

Minimum Educational Requirements
None

Personal Qualities
Optimistic; risk-taker; curious; passion for the business; physical stamina

Certification and Licensing
Depends on job

Working Conditions
Depends on job

Salary Range
About $31,000 to more than $100,000 per year in 2016

Number of Jobs
29,600,000 in 2016

Future Job Outlook
Optimistic

trepreneurs include those who create businesses that operate online, out of the owner's home, or on an individual freelance basis. For a person who has an idea for a business, and the determination to make it happen, owning a small business can be a rewarding career as well as a vital contribution to the US economy.

Running a small business requires a wide range of knowledge and skills. "As a small business owner, you're used to doing it all," says entrepreneur Mike Kappel on the *Forbes* business website. "You built your business from the ground up. And, every day your business continues because of the things you do and the choices you make." Before opening a small business, the owner must first develop a business plan, which is a written description of the prospective business: what it is, what products it makes or sells, how it will make a profit, and what the expected future of the business is. The business plan is used to obtain financing for a start-up business, attract investors, and serve as a sort of roadmap for operating the business. A small business owner is not likely to secure a business loan from a bank without a convincing business plan.

Once the firm is up and running, the daily tasks of operating a business begin. The basic tasks performed by the small business owner are usually the same as those in large corporations. Managing inventory to make sure there is enough product to sell is a primary responsibility. If the business does not manufacture its own products, the small business owner must keep close contact with suppliers to make sure that there is adequate inventory, and place orders when needed. If the business deals in a service, the owner must make sure there are enough employees to handle jobs as they are booked. The small business owner performs accounting duties, such as pricing merchandise, creating budgets, monitoring cash flow, and keeping an accurate set of records. Marketing is another important aspect, which may entail maintaining a website, placing advertisements in local media, creating brochures and other print material, and sending press releases to newspapers and broadcast media.

If the business has employees, the owner must hire, train, and supervise the workers. He or she must explain workplace rules and practices, such as working hours, the availability of overtime, and benefits such as sick leave. Employee competency must be monitored and may lead to one of the more unpleasant duties of a small business owner: firing an unsatisfactory worker. Along with employee relations, customer relations are a key ingredient to the success of a small business. Customer relations involve making sure that customers are treated as an important part of the business. Visitors to a store must be made to feel welcome and appreciated, and complaints or merchandise returns should be handled honestly and willingly.

Building and operating a small business requires an enormous amount of dedication, ingenuity, and hard work. Sometimes even those qualities are not enough for success: about half of new small businesses close after only five years. But for the half that succeeds in the long run, the rewards for the small business owners are abundant: career satisfaction, pride of ownership, the opportunity for financial and personal freedom, and a sense of independence that cannot be duplicated in a corporate setting.

How Do You Become a Small Business Owner?

Education

There is no formal educational requirement for becoming a small business owner. Practically speaking, however, a high school diploma can be considered the minimum education for people who want to start their own business. Courses in English, math, and such business skills as accounting or bookkeeping, if available, are helpful. A college degree with a major or minor in business administration, finance, accounting, or other business disciplines is also a valuable basis for a small business owner. For people who wish to set up their own professional business, such as an independent accountant, a family counselor, or an attorney, a thorough education in their respective field is essential.

Several government and nonprofit organizations exist to help the small business owner develop the skills necessary for a successful enterprise. Among these are the SBA and SCORE, which stands for Service Corps of Retired Executives (although it is known by its acronym).

Certification and Licensing

In general, a small business owner will need a license to operate his or her business. These licenses are usually obtained from the city or county in which the business operates. The need for specific certification or special licensing depends on the requirements of the business. A small business that deals with food preparation or vending, for example, must obtain a license from the local health department. Businesses selling such items as liquor, gasoline, or firearms will need a state-issued license, and some occupations—including those in real estate, insurance, cosmetology, and medical services—must also be licensed. Professional occupations, such as certified public accountants, physicians, and architects, require their own educational and certification requirements.

Volunteer Work and Internships

Many small businesses have internship programs that can help a student gain practical knowledge of a particular business. Some internships are paid, although small businesses with limited budgets may offer unpaid internships, which have restrictions on the kind of work an intern may perform. Small business owners act as mentors, giving interns the benefits of their knowledge and experience.

Skills and Personality

Successful small business owners have mastered the basic business skills that are important for any company. Leadership and communication skills allow the small business owner to effectively handle the day-to-day interactions with his or her employees and customers. Math skills are necessary to make sure that the business is operating within its budget and has enough capital to cover both ordinary and unforeseen expenses. Sales and marketing skills are valuable, as is an up-to-date knowledge of emerging technology.

When first getting started, many small business owners work out of their homes to keep expenses low. Developing a business plan and obtaining financing are two important steps in becoming a successful business owner.

The small business owner must be passionate about the business and optimistic about its chances for success. Marketing consultant Carolyn Higgins writes on the Fortune Marketing Company website, "I don't think a pessimist can succeed as a small business owner. There is too much that will go wrong and too many hurdles to overcome." Not being afraid to take risks is also essential in a business environment where success is not a certainty. "Nothing great was ever built by playing it safe," says Higgins. "If you want your small business to thrive you absolutely have to be able to take risks and do things that make you nervous once in a while."

Finally, the owner must have an abundance of energy and stamina; running a small business is not the easiest way to make a living, but it can be one of the most rewarding for those who have the skills and personality to make it work.

On the Job

Employers

One of the reasons small business owners go into business for themselves is the desire to work without having to report to an employer. Financial expert Holly Johnson, who left her regular job to become her own boss, writes on the WiseBread website,

> Even though self-employment isn't perfect, I couldn't imagine going back to a regular job now. I truly enjoy the challenge of figuring out how to earn a living without a steady salary. I am used to putting my head down and working hard to achieve my goals without having to make small talk or drive to an office. And I love the fact I can earn more money by working harder, instead of relying on someone else to determine how much money I make.

Working Conditions

For small business owners, working conditions are as varied as the types of businesses are. Work settings can range from an accountant's or counselor's office in the home to such businesses as roofing installation, landscaping, or house painting, where employees labor outdoors in all kinds of weather. Some businesses can be managed solely by the owner, but others require teamwork to get the job done. Working hours also vary, but most small business owners tend to work longer hours than those employed by firms. A 2017 Small Business Pulse Survey revealed that 84 percent of business owners regularly worked more than forty hours per week, and 10 percent of them felt overwhelmed by their responsibilities. Getting time away from the job is harder for the self-employed as well: only 57 percent of small business owners planned to take a vacation. And two-thirds of those vacationing owners will check in with work at least once a day.

Earnings

Small business owners' earnings vary widely depending on several factors. Overall, a 2011 survey by the website PayScale reports that annual salaries ranged from $38,568 to $91,440. Additional income from bonuses, commissions, and profit sharing can increase these figures. Amount of experience can also affect earnings: owners with less than four years of experience earn from $31,116 to $73,250, whereas those with more than twenty years in the business can make nearly $100,000 annually. Other factors affecting earnings include the state in which the business operates (California has top earnings), the industry (construction is the most profitable), and the owner's gender (men make more than women.)

Opportunities for Advancement

While job advancement in the traditional sense of climbing the corporate ladder may not apply to a small business owner, there are opportunities to advance in the small business world. If a business is growing and there are sufficient funds available, a small business owner may decide to expand by adding new product lines, opening a second location, or establishing an online presence. Partnering with a similar business can bring in new customers, as can modifying a product to target a new market segment.

What Is the Future Outlook for Small Business Owners?

The outlook for small business is optimistic. According to Mark Abell on the Biznet website, "Small business optimism has spiked since the election of Donald Trump . . . [and is] driven by expectations of a strong economy and rising incomes, lower taxes, strong consumer sentiment, and rising home prices." As of April 2018, 21 percent of small business owners expected higher sales, 61 percent were spending money to improve their businesses, and 57 percent had increased hiring.

Find Out More

Service Corps of Retired Executives (SCORE)
1175 Herndon Pkwy., Suite 900
Herndon, VA 20170
website: www.score.org

SCORE offers mentoring services to new and established small businesses, as well as free seminars, online courses, and other educational resources.

SmartBiz
website: www.smartbiz.com

This website offers information on all aspects of small businesses, including technology and Internet, accounting, human resources, taxes, and more. It includes downloadable business forms, a blog, and e-mail newsletters.

TheSelfEmployed.com
website: www.theselfemployed.com

TheSelfEmployed.com contains resources for self-employed and small business owners, including articles, how-to videos, podcasts, forums, and special offers that are all designed specifically for the self-employed.

US Small Business Administration (SBA)
409 Third St. SW
Washington, DC 20416
website: www.sba.gov

The SBA provides counseling for small businesses and helps with securing financing, writing business plans, performing market research, and dealing with human resource issues.

Financial Analyst

What Does a Financial Analyst Do?

When an individual or company decides to invest money in a stock, bond, or business, a great deal of research must be done to ensure that the investment will be a sound one. The role of the financial analyst (sometimes called a securities analyst or investment analyst) is to perform this research, analyze the data, and make investment recommendations through written reports or in-person meetings with clients or managers. Brady Raanes, the director of investment strategy at Raanes Capital Advisors, describes his daily routine in Kaplan University's booklet *Getting There from Here: Career Path Stories from Finance Professionals*.

There's not really an average day in my line of work. . . . Probably 60% of my day is reactive. A client calls and wants to meet, or I am responding to voicemails and emails. The other 40% of the day is planned activities. I come in and read

At a Glance

Financial Analyst

Minimum Educational Requirements
Bachelor's degree

Personal Qualities
Creative thinking; flexibility; problem solving; detail oriented

Certification and Licensing
Not required, but helpful for advancement

Working Conditions
Office environment with some travel

Salary Range
About $51,780 to $165,580 per year in 2016

Number of Jobs
296,100 in 2016

Future Job Outlook
Projected 11 percent growth through 2026, which is faster than average

news headlines and skim stock headlines, to try to figure out what the markets are doing. If I see anything that jumps out to me, I do a screen of which accounts we manage that hold the stock. Once a month, I review our financial models and allocations, and determine if anything needs to be changed.

Financial analysts assess the performance of stocks and bonds and evaluate current business trends. If the analyst works for a financial consulting firm, these tasks are performed for outside clients. Analysts may also work for a company, performing analytical research for presentation to the firm's upper management. By studying past and present financial data, analysts investigate the stock company's records to determine whether it would be a suitable investment for the analyst's firm or client. The financial analyst's research is often focused on a specific industry or product. As business becomes more global, a financial analyst may specialize in a particular country or region of the world. This entails learning about international relations, foreign economies, and different political systems to gauge how markets and stock performances are influenced by these factors.

After investigating a stock company's financial information, analysts create reports for their own managers or clients on potential investments, develop budgets and analyze cash flow, and ensure compliance with tax and other regulations. Using sophisticated software to evaluate raw financial data is an important part of the financial analyst's job. Ezgi Bereketli, who provides web data for investors, stresses the importance of data on the *Forbes* website:

> It is no secret that data has become a prerequisite for analysis, as the digitized world has enabled our every movement to be translated into data points captured by various technologies. The unstoppable and ever-growing expansion of the data universe, coupled with an increasing appreciation of the capabilities of sophisticated data analysis, has made the data analyst the magician of our time.

Such software makes the financial analyst's job easier and more accurate. But software is just a tool: it is the conclusions that financial analysts draw from the data and their expertise that make them valuable to their clients. That expertise may be directed into one of numerous areas in which the financial analyst can specialize. Risk analysts evaluate the risks of various investments to minimize losses. Ratings analysts investigate a company's financial health to determine its ability to repay its debts. Credit analysts evaluate the creditworthiness of a company or organization, and investment analysts recommend suitable investments. Tax analysts prepare tax filings for a company or client and keep informed of the latest changes in tax law. In a small firm, one person may be tasked with duties under several of these specialties, but larger firms are more likely to have an analyst concentrate on one area of responsibility.

A career as a financial analyst can be challenging, exciting, and financially rewarding. But job satisfaction involves more than monetary gain. As financial adviser Drew Harmon relates in *Getting There from Here*, "My favorite part of my job is the results. It's seeing a client after I have helped them identify a problem and craft a solution that best suits them now and in the future. Seeing their confidence build and their worry go away is very rewarding."

How Do You Become a Financial Analyst?

Education

A bachelor's degree in such fields as economics, statistics, finance, or accounting is required for most financial analyst positions. Sometimes a degree in other areas may be acceptable if an aptitude in mathematics or other areas relevant to financial analysis can be demonstrated. Some firms offer in-house training for entry-level financial analysts. Another avenue for education is the availability of local or online courses that can help develop or improve knowledge of analytic software, international trade regulations, tax law, and other relevant subjects.

Certification and Licensing

Obtaining a chartered financial analyst (CFA) credential is often recommended by employers. Sponsored by the CFA Institute, the certification indicates that a financial analyst has demonstrated a strong knowledge of the financial profession. A bachelor's degree and four years of professional work experience are required to take the CFA exams, which are given in three increasing levels of difficulty. The Association for Financial Professionals also conducts a program for certifying a financial analyst as a financial planning and analysis professional. These certifications can help a financial analyst move up in his or her career path.

Financial analysts who deal with sales of securities (investments such as stocks, bonds, and mutual funds) must be registered by the Financial Industry Regulatory Authority (FINRA), the main licensing organization for the securities industry. FINRA administers a variety of qualifying exams to test a financial analyst's competence in his or her specialization.

Volunteer Work and Internships

Juniors and seniors in high school or students in college who have had classes in economics or other business subjects may be able to obtain volunteer positions in finance. Nonprofit organizations and small businesses that have limited budgets often rely on volunteer help with bookkeeping and other business-related areas. Such opportunities can be beneficial for building a résumé and gaining firsthand knowledge in the field.

Summer internships are often available with banks and other financial institutions. Internships help develop varied skills in finance and client services and are a good means of networking with individuals in the industry. Some internships may ultimately lead to an offer of full-time employment.

Derek was a senior at Howard University when he interned as an analyst at investment banking firm Goldman Sachs in New York City. "I think of working at Goldman Sachs as more than just a job. . . . " Derek notes on the company's website, "The firm has an abundance of resources, so whenever I have some down time, I study, read and practice to increase my knowledge and widen my skill set. In addition, I feel that each day I am forming stronger bonds with my intern class."

Skills and Personality

A financial analyst must first and foremost have excellent math and data interpretation skills and be comfortable with computer technology and the latest software, both specialized financial programs and general software such as word processing, presentation, and database. Because working with large amounts of financial data is required, a financial analyst must be organized and experienced in planning and setting goals, often under the pressure of project deadlines.

The financial analyst must have good written and oral communication skills to present findings to clients or employees at all levels of a corporation. "Communication abilities are vital for financial analysts, as are other soft skills," says Greg Lainas, the senior vice president for Robert Half Management Resources, on the company website. Soft skills are personality traits such as creative thinking, motivation, flexibility, and conflict resolution that can make a person more valuable in his or her job. "In fact," Lainas continues, "these skills can be a deciding factor in the hiring process when an employer is evaluating two candidates with similar technical skills."

A successful financial analyst will have the kind of personality that is both detail oriented and shows an aptitude for solving problems. Being comfortable working either independently or as part of a team is a plus, as is being a self-starter and having the willingness to take on increasing levels of responsibility.

On the Job

Employers

Financial analysts typically work in such finance-related fields as banking, insurance, financial management, pension and fund management, and brokerage and investment. Many large corporations and government agencies also employ financial analysts. Many financial analysts work as independent advisers, building their own lists of clients.

Although jobs for financial analysts can be found in smaller cities, major urban hubs offer the most opportunities for employment. Financial districts such as Wall Street in New York City and LaSalle Street in Chicago are major areas for those looking for employment as a financial analyst.

Working Conditions

Most financial analysts work in an office setting, but independent financial analysts usually work from a home office or leased office space. Travel is often required to meet clients. An unnamed financial analyst who works with mutual funds talks about his job on the website CityTownInfo:

> [I] travel a lot to meet with company CEOs at conferences and at their offices. The job is highly intellectual. Working with very smart people is a big plus. Every day there is something new to learn, new industries to discover and interesting people to meet. Variety and intellectual challenge make this job very interesting. The toughest part of the job is keeping up with a lot of information and long days.

Balancing work and home life may be challenging for new financial analysts. While most financial analysts work a forty-hour week, the first few years of employment may require more, sometimes as much as seventy to eighty hours per week. In addition, working during off-hours to network and research market trends can also cut into a person's free time. Many financial analysts experience high levels of stress and fatigue in their early years on the job.

Earnings

The financial analyst's long hours and hard work are compensated by substantial monetary rewards. According to the Bureau of Labor

Statistics (BLS), the median annual salary for financial analysts in 2016 was $81,760. The lowest 10 percent received less than $51,780, and the highest 10 percent earned more than $165,580. Such generous compensation makes the field highly competitive.

Opportunities for Advancement

Those just entering the field with a bachelor's degree usually begin their careers as a junior analyst. With the earning of a master's degree in business administration or finance, they may advance to a senior analyst position having more decision-making responsibilities. With additional experience, the senior financial analyst may become a portfolio manager for corporate investments or a fund manager handling investments for individual clients. In a large corporation, a talented senior financial analyst may rise to an upper management position, including chief financial officer.

What Is the Future Outlook for Financial Analysts?

The BLS projects employment growth of 11 percent for financial analysts through 2026, which is a fast growth rate compared to all other occupations. In a growing economy, the demand for financial analysts will increase as new businesses are established and technological advances provide more precise financial data for analysts to study.

Find Out More

American Finance Association (AFA)
website: https://afajof.site-ym.com

The American Finance Association is the premier academic organization devoted to the study and promotion of knowledge about financial economics. The AFA website lists jobs in academia, the finance industry, and in government. It publishes the

Journal of Finance and sponsors student poster competitions at its annual meeting.

American Management Association (AMA)
1601 Broadway
New York, NY 10019
website: www.amanet.org

The American Management Association offers educational programs, conferences, online training, and publications for professionals working in various aspects of human resources. The AMA offers specially selected programs in analytical skills, including developing critical thinking, fundamentals of data analysis, and financial forecasting.

Association for Financial Professionals (AFP)
4520 East-West Hwy., Suite 800
Bethesda, MD 20814
website: www.afponline.org

This organization is dedicated to advancing the success of people in the financial professions. It offers professional certification in corporate financial planning and analysis and hosts the largest annual networking conference in the field. Its website offers a magazine, newsletters, survey research and data, and information on career development.

CFA Institute
915 E. High St.
Charlottesville, VA 22902
website: www.cfainstitute.org

The CFA Institute is the leading organization for investment management professionals. It develops and administers best practice guidelines and standards that guide the investment industry. The institute has free resources for students and works with educational institutions to promote the highest standards of ethics, education, and professional excellence.

Public Relations Specialist

At a Glance

Public Relations Specialist

Minimum Educational Requirements
Bachelor's degree

Personal Qualities
Communication skills; public speaking; creativity; computer skills; attention to detail

Certification and Licensing
Not required

Working Conditions
Office environment, with some off-site activities

Salary Range
About $32,840 to $112,260 per year in 2016

Number of Jobs
259,600 in 2016

Future Job Outlook
Projected increase of 9 percent through 2026, which is about average

What Does a Public Relations Specialist Do?

When a business or organization wants to put its best face forward to the world, it calls on a public relations specialist to do the job. For virtually all types of businesses, whether commercial or nonprofit, favorable public relations are essential to fashion their public image and promote awareness of their products, activities, or goals.

The public relations specialist is the link between a company or outside client and the public. These professionals perform a variety of tasks, most of which are closely tied to written, oral, and media communication. For example, they might write press releases for distribution to the media and craft speeches to be delivered by company executives. Public relations specialists write copy for radio and local and national television broadcasts, and they keep in contact with these outlets on behalf of their organizations or clients. A public relations specialist's job may also include damage control and finding ways to shed a favorable light on a company's mistakes, such as the recall of a faulty product or a scandal involving a high-ranking executive. Therefore, checking news stories about a client and following social media are important areas in which the public relations specialist must keep current.

Public relations work is often varied, but many public relations specialists concentrate on a specific area. Lisa Hess, who specializes in placing clients on broadcast media, talks about her typical day in an article on the public relations website News and Experts:

> I usually get in by 8:25 a.m. and go through my emails and answer anything urgent. Then, I go into our staff meeting where I have a chance to discuss my plan for the day, based on the campaigns I have in the works, and review new pitches that have to get written in order to have a successful week.
>
> Right after the meeting, I check out news headlines to see if any of our national TV clients match what is going on in the news. If they do, I contact the client immediately, asking for their comments, so that we can put together a pitch and get it out by noon at the latest. Any later than noon and I'll miss the window to get it in front of producers.
>
> Next I follow up on any media responses that might have come in overnight and answer any urgent client emails. After that, I choose which clients to work on for local TV appearances, based on the time zone and the dates the client is to be in that town.

Some public relations specialists handle special events, such as promoting company anniversaries, arranging press conferences, and coordinating educational seminars and fund-raisers. Public relations specialist Sandee Hart of the web-development company ParadoxLabs discusses the role of public relations in special events on the company's website:

In the world of public relations, a planned event is the stage where a business must perform. . . . Personally, I tend to take on the role of the director when working on an event. I take this job seriously because it is my job to ensure each attendee achieves the organization's goals and objectives. This often means managing, controlling, and influencing multiple aspects of the event. . . . As a public relations specialist, it is my job to establish and maintain relationships with our target audience, the media, and stakeholders.

During the twenty-first century, social media platforms have changed almost every aspect of life, and public relations is no exception. Facebook, Twitter, and other platforms have become important outlets for determining the interests of consumers, establishing professional relationships, and promoting businesses. The public relations specialist must understand how people use social media and know how to integrate traditional public relations methods with the new media. "Social media does not replace traditional media," says public relations expert and author Amy Howell on the public relations website Cision. "Traditional media is still very important, when paired with social media, it's even more powerful."

The public relations specialist is an important part of a company's efforts to disseminate information about its successes, new discoveries or products, and advances that benefit not only its own industry, but society as well. It is a career filled with challenges, a variety of areas in which to work, and opportunities to creatively enhance the image a business needs to succeed.

How Do You Become a Public Relations Specialist?

Education

A bachelor's degree is the minimum educational requirement for most positions in public relations. Courses of study should include business administration, communication, journalism, management, and English. The most common degree for public relations specialists is a degree in communication: about 15 percent of public relations specialists majored in communication. Many colleges and universities offer a major or minor concentration in public relations. Students in these programs usually create a portfolio of creative work to show to prospective employers. Colleges that do not award degrees in public relations may offer individual courses related to the field, often as a part of other departments such as communication or journalism.

Entry-level public relations specialists may receive on-the-job training, which can last up to a year in many firms. During this period, new hires learn about the company and perform basic tasks such as maintaining files and searching media for information relating to the company's industry. Many public relations specialists obtain a master's degree to become public relations managers.

Certification and Licensing

Certification is not required of public relations specialists, but it can be an important way to demonstrate competence in the field. The Public Relations Society of America (PRSA) awards the Accredited in Public Relations (APR) credential to specialists who have demonstrated knowledge and competency in the field. A candidate for the APR credential must study areas of public relations, prepare a portfolio of work for an in-person presentation, and complete a computer-based examination. The PRSA recommends a minimum of five years' experience in public relations prior to applying for certification.

Volunteer Work and Internships

Internships provide students with valuable experience in many areas of the public relations field. Experience in an area of communication, such as editing or writing for a school newspaper, can help a student secure a summer position. Interns may be asked to perform tasks such as monitoring news media and writing reports. Chelsea Quinlan, who interned at the public relations firm Weber Shandwick in Seattle, Washington, describes her experience on the company website:

> I'm an intern for Weber Shandwick's Global Technology team. In short, our team oversees all tech work across the agency. . . . Overall, there is not a "typical day" for me. There are tasks I do daily such as responding to emails, and often updating team lists for the technology practice, but my days really vary based on what the agency needs. It's my job to stay flexible and I enjoy that aspect of agency life because it keeps my work exciting and interesting, presenting an abundance of new opportunities to learn about our industry.

Skills and Personality

A public relations specialist's most important skill is an expertise in communication. He or she must be comfortable with speaking in public, whether it is to an individual executive, a gathering of media representatives, or a roomful of people. Proficiency in written communication is also vital for creating press releases, brochures, broadcast copy, or social media content. Effective communicating means not only having skills in speaking and writing but also the ability to listen and relate to people from all walks of life.

Another important skill is the ability to think creatively when crafting speeches and written content and when developing unique promotional campaigns for clients. Being organized and exhibiting excellent time-management skills are essential traits for handling multiple projects with various clients, often at the same time. Having a thick skin can help specialists deal with rejection, which is an unavoidable part of the public relations business. Public relations specialists must be flexible in their thinking and become adept at proposing new concepts when a client rejects a particular idea.

As technology advances, good computer skills are essential for writing, creating presentations, and performing research. It is also an advantage to think globally as the economy becomes more dependent on penetrating international markets. Finally, being detail oriented and a proponent of accuracy—via editing, proofreading, and fact checking—will prevent an embarrassing mistake from making its way into a press release or media story.

On the Job

Employers

There were about 259,600 public relations specialists working in the field in 2016. Many of them work in public relations departments in large corporations, but others work for independent public relations firms that provide services to outside clients. The majority of public relations specialists work for advertising and public relations firms, followed by educational institutions, businesses, and government agencies.

Working Conditions

Public relations specialists normally work in an office environment. Full-time working hours range typically from thirty-five to forty hours a week, although overtime is often required. Evening and weekend work devoted to attending meetings and other events is not uncommon. Much time may be spent away from the office entertaining clients, meeting with the media, and supervising special events.

Although the popular view of public relations is often tinged with the excitement of socializing with industry elites and attending gala promotions, the day-to-day duties can be difficult and stressful. "Agency life will be draining, daunting, and often thankless," says public relations specialist Nicole Messier on the website PR Daily. "If you want to be the next undiscovered talent—or the young professional with the corner office—you have to work your butt off to get there."

Earnings

The Bureau of Labor Statistics (BLS) reports that the median annual salary for a public relations specialist in 2016 was $58,020. The highest-paid specialists earned more than $112,260, and the lowest paid earned less than $32,840. Public relations specialists working in government earned a median salary of $62,400 per year, and those in educational services received $53,840.

Opportunities for Advancement

Entry-level public relations specialists can expect to be given assignments with limited responsibility. After gaining several years' experience, the specialist is given more responsibility with a corresponding higher salary. A master's degree in public relations or a communication-related field, and APR certification, can lead to a management position. Many public relations specialists change jobs to gain the best opportunities for advancement, but others may achieve the goal of opening their own public relations firm.

What Is the Future Outlook for Public Relations Specialists?

The need for public relations specialists will grow about as fast as average according to the BLS, which projects a 9 percent increase in public relations jobs through 2026. As the Internet increasingly spreads information—both good and bad—that can affect public opinion about businesses, the need for public relations specialists has increased. There will, however, be stiff competition for entry-level public relations jobs as more communication majors seek employment in public relations.

Find Out More

International Association of Business Communicators (IABC)
155 Montgomery St., Suite 1210
San Francisco, CA 94104
website: www.iabc.org.

The IABC is a global organization devoted to improving business communication. It offers online workshops for career growth, networking opportunities, and an annual conference. Student members can take advantage of the organization's job and internship center.

National Communication Association (NCA)
1765 N St. NW
Washington, DC 20036
website: www.natcom.org

The National Communication Association promotes professionalism in communication in many disciplines, from academic to business. The organization publishes academic journals and provides data on jobs and education in communication. The NCA Career Center provides students with resources for academic employment in the field.

Public Relations Society of America (PRSA)
120 Wall St.
New York, NY 10005
website: www.prsa.org

The Public Relations Society of America is the largest organization serving public relations and communication professionals. The PRSA offers resources for advancing professional development in public relations. It provides the Public Relations Bootcamp, which provides information for the new or prospective public relations specialist.

Public Relations Student Society of America (PRSSA)
120 Wall St.
New York, NY 10005
website: www.prssa.org

The PRSSA is the student-oriented organization of the PRSA. It helps public relations students network with professionals in the field and provides information via blogs, a newspaper, and through social media. The organization gives students hands-on experience through its student-run firms, which work with outside clients.

Sales Engineer

What Does a Sales Engineer Do?

For a person who is comfortable with complex science and high-tech machines and also enjoys meeting and talking to a variety of people, the job of sales engineer may just be the path to a fulfilling career. A sales engineer combines these two disciplines by presenting technical solutions that address a prospective business customer's needs and then making sure that the process of system design, installation, and implementation of the products are accomplished to the customer's satisfaction. In this respect, a sales engineer's job differs from that of a salesperson who works in retail businesses selling goods to consumers. Engineering sales is a business-to-business venture in which the customers are usually corporations, scientific organizations, government agencies, or other large organizations.

Sales engineers begin with initial meetings with customers to determine what products will best fill a company's technical requirements. Such products may include computer systems, telecommunications

At a Glance

Sales Engineer

Minimum Educational Requirements
Bachelor's degree in an engineering or science discipline

Personal Qualities
Interest in technology; good interpersonal skills; outgoing personality; strong communication skills

Certification and Licensing
Not required

Working Conditions
Office environment with frequent travel

Salary Range
About $56,940 to $162,740 per year in 2016

Number of Jobs
74,900 as of 2016

Future Job Outlook
Projected growth of 7 percent through 2026, which is about average

networks, automated manufacturing tools, scientific instruments, and more. Depending on the nature of the products involved, the sales engineer may meet with the customer's engineering staff to work out technical details. Then he or she will prepare a proposal for the client, often working with other members of the sales staff. The sales engineer presents the proposal to the client.

Once the sale is complete and contracts are signed, the sales engineer monitors the progress of fulfilling the order, making sure the correct equipment is assembled and deadlines are met. After the equipment is installed at the customer's facility, the sales engineer instructs the customer in the operation and maintenance of the equipment. The sales engineer will also troubleshoot any problems that may arise after installation and make sure that the system is working properly. Follow-up calls, either by phone or in person, allow the sales engineer to make sure the customer is satisfied and present an opportunity to discuss other products that may interest the customer.

Akin Edwards was a software developer and information technology (IT) administrator who became a sales engineer. He discusses his job on the IT company Okta's website:

> I've always loved challenging myself and learning from those challenges, and I am constantly challenged technically in this role. As a sales engineer, the possibilities are limitless. . . . I am typically brought into meetings by my colleagues to perform product demos, whiteboard architecture, implement a proof of concept, and begin working with customers in order to streamline their IT landscape. I want them to feel completely comfortable with their unique configuration and set them up for success. When I'm not working with customers, I'm collaborating with the team and acting as a liaison between Okta's internal divisions. My goal internally is to distill technical information and help collaborative teams work on customer projects.

A sales engineer may often work with a team of sales representatives. "As technologies become more complex, so do the means by which those technologies are sold," says market researcher Ken Presti on the Cisco company blog. "Expertise varies, and there is a point at which sales efforts are conducted in teams consisting of a sales rep who deals with the contractual element, and the sales engineer who handles the technical heavy-lifting." Another means of customer contact for the sales engineer is the Internet. For example, SmartBear, a software development company headquartered in Somerville, Massachusetts, uses webinars to educate customers and showcase new products with its online SmartBear Academy.

Part of a sales engineer's job may be to perform market research to identify potential customers. Once a possible customer is identified, the sales engineer will make cold calls, which are unsolicited contacts, to introduce his or her company and promote their services or products. Along with the sales side of the job, a sales engineer may also work with his or her company's engineering team to carry out technical research to help in the development of new products.

According to Okta's Edwards, being a sales engineer is rewarding because he is "helping organizations adopt best-in-class technology and making it easier for organizations that are stuck on old technology . . . to get on the same playing field as their industry's leaders."

How Do You Become a Sales Engineer?

Education

The minimum educational requirement for most sales engineer jobs is a bachelor's degree, usually in engineering. Prospective employers look for people with a degree in the discipline that relates to the job opening, such as electrical, mechanical, or chemical engineering. Often a degree in a related technical field (such as computer science) or one of the physical or natural sciences (such as biology, physics, or chemistry) may also be appropriate for an entry-level engineering position. Having a minor concentration in business, communication, or English can be helpful in preparing for the sales side of the job.

According to the Bureau of Labor Statistics (BLS), in some instances people who have extensive experience in sales as well as technical experience or training could become sales engineers without the traditional requirement of a degree. In these cases, companies provide on-the-job training to familiarize the new sales engineer with the firm's business practices and organization.

Certification and Licensing

Certification is not required for sales engineers, but it can enhance one's professional standing. There are several voluntary training courses that lead to certification. The National Association of Sales Professionals offers a six-week course in modern sales techniques that culminates in the Certified Professional Sales Person credential. The Certified Manufacturing Technology Sales Engineer credential confirms the experience and knowledge of sales engineers who work in manufacturing technology, and meSE, a global leader in sales engineering education, offers the Sales Engineer Certification, which attests to proficiency in sales and customer relations skills.

Volunteer Work and Internships

Internships are a great way to gain knowledge, experience, and professional contacts for the prospective sales engineer. Interns usually begin performing low-responsibility tasks such as handling customer requests and basic marketing assignments. With more experience, interns may conduct cold sales calls and go on client visits with sales engineers.

As a university student in India, sales engineer Akshay Karthik completed four internships at both large and small companies. On Medium, a social journalism website, he says his experiences "helped me to understand my strengths and urged me to learn more. . . . After completing my internship with SPI Incubator I was confident and clear about what I want to do and what job helps me to do that. In my campus placements I got selected . . . as a Pre Sales Engineer." Karthik says he gained skills in networking, multitasking, and communicating with people during his internships.

Skills and Personality

Two main personality traits may define the successful sales engineer: the ability to cultivate good interpersonal relationships and an active interest in science and technology. Strong interpersonal skills help the sales engineer to understand client needs and clearly communicate solutions to those needs, and technical knowledge is necessary to determine the appropriate technology to offer a client. Sales presentations are a major part of the job, not only to individual customers but also at such venues as trade shows and conferences. The ability to speak in public and refine complex technologies into easily understandable terms is an asset for the sales engineer.

An outgoing personality and the ability to project confidence are personality traits that the prospective sales engineer should nurture. Likewise, a creative mind helps the sales engineer to develop unique solutions for a customer's technical requirements. Other important traits include problem-solving, organizational and time-management skills, as well as the ability to set priorities to ensure that the most critical concerns are addressed.

On the Job

Employers

According to the BLS, most sales engineers work for merchant wholesalers, manufacturing companies, computer system design firms, electronic wholesalers, and telecommunications companies. A sales engineer working for a manufacturer will concentrate on selling the company's products. Sales engineers may also work for a systems design and integration firm or as independent consultants, representing products from a variety of manufacturers.

Working Conditions

The usual work schedule for a sales engineer is forty hours per week, but overtime is often required when creating complex systems proposals or working to meet tight sales deadlines. The BLS reports that as many as one-third of sales engineers worked more than forty hours a week in 2016. Working hours can often be irregular, especially if a customer is in a different time zone or a foreign country.

Sales engineers generally spend much of their time in an office environment contacting clients, researching products for customers, working with both sales and engineering coworkers, and creating sales proposals. The rest of their time is spent on the road, visiting clients and making sales presentations. Many sales engineers are responsible for covering assigned sales territories and thus may be away from the office for days or even weeks at a time, depending on the size of the territory.

While travel is a necessary part of the job, being away from home for extended periods can be stressful for the sales engineer and his or her family. Stress can also be a component of making cold calls or presenting complicated information to a customer who may be unfamiliar with the technology.

Earnings

According to the BLS, sales engineers earned a median annual salary of $100,000 in 2016. The lowest 10 percent made less than $56,940, and the highest 10 percent earned more than $162,740. Sales engineers in telecommunication made the most money, followed by those in computer systems design, wholesale electronics, and manufacturing.

Most sales engineers work for salary plus commission, in which the base income is augmented by payments of a percentage of the value of each sale made. Sometimes lump-sum bonuses are paid in place of a commission. Thus, a sales engineer's earnings can vary widely from year to year based on changes in sales performance, the state of the economy, and the demand for a company's products. Commissions or bonuses may be paid monthly, quarterly, or annually, and they may make up 10 to 25 percent or more of a sales engineer's total earnings. Some independent sales engineers work on commission only.

Opportunities for Advancement

While there is no standard career path for a sales engineer, advancement is possible. With a few years of experience and a good sales record, a sales engineer may become a senior sales engineer, earning higher commissions or bonuses, and perhaps being assigned a larger sales territory. For sales engineers seeking more responsibility, going into management is a goal worth pursuing. John Care, managing director of Mastering Technical Sales, a company dedicated to skills development for sales engineers, says in an article entitled "The Sales Engineer Career Path: Now What?", that 39 percent of sales engineers see managing other sales engineers as the next step in their careers. This could eventually lead to upper-level management positions, including the vice president of sales or even the chief executive officer.

What Is the Future Outlook for Sales Engineers?

The BLS estimates that employment for sales engineers will grow 7 percent through 2026, which is about average compared to all occupations. A major factor that will affect the number of sales engineer job openings is the ongoing development of new scientific and technological products, especially in the area of computer technology. As more companies outsource their sales operations, opportunities for independent sales engineers and consultants will increase.

Find Out More

Manufacturers' Agents National Association (MANA)
6321 W. Dempster St., Suite 110
Morton Grove, IL 60053
website: www.manaonline.org

MANA is a trade organization representing manufacturers' agents, including sales engineers, in various industries. It publishes a monthly online and printed magazine, a blog, and podcasts on various areas of sales.

Manufacturers' Representatives Educational Research Foundation
5460 Ward Rd., Suite 125
Arvada, CO 80002
website: https://mrerf.org

This organization offers the Certified Professional Manufacturers Representative credential for professional outside sales representatives. It also provides educational resources for both manufacturers and their individual representatives, and it promotes the importance of the manufacturer and representative relationship.

National Association of Sales Professionals (NASP)
8300 N. Hayden Rd., Suite 207
Scottsdale, AZ 85258
website: www.nasp.org

NASP is the largest online community of sales professionals. It offers online training courses and webinars of interest to the sales professional, and its career center provides up-to-date employment information to members.

Top Sales World
website: https://topsalesworld.com

The motto of this professional sales website is "Inspiring the global sales community." It offers numerous resources for sales specialists or those considering sales careers, including a monthly online sales magazine and back-issue archive, weekly sales articles and posts, links to marketing blogs, and audio interviews with sales professionals.

Franchise Owner

At a Glance

Franchise Owner

Minimum Educational Requirements
None

Personal Qualities
Business skills; communication and interpersonal skills; leadership; team player

Certification and Licensing
Franchisor certification and business licenses may be required

Working Conditions
Depends on the type of business

Salary Range
About $10,000 to more than $250,000 per year in 2016, depending on numerous factors

Number of Jobs
745,290 franchise outlets in the United States (some owners own multiple units)

Future Job Outlook
Predicted to grow by approximately 1.7 percent, depending on changes in the economy

What Does a Franchise Owner Do?

A franchise owner (also known as the franchisee) buys the rights to operate a business as part of a larger company (the franchisor) to use that company's name and sell its products or services. For example, McDonald's, Subway, and KFC are just a few of the numerous fast-food franchise opportunities available for a person with a solid business sense and an inclination toward discipline and hard work.

The franchise owner can operate his or her business in one of several ways. Some franchise owners take an active role in the everyday aspects of the business, working alongside the employees and interacting with customers while also performing management duties. Other owners, especially those who own multiple stores, hire managers to handle the day-to-day tasks, while the owner regularly visits the various locations to observe their operation and deal with any problems. Some franchises can be operated out of a home office or other residential space. Whatever business model is used, the work of a franchise owner is diverse and demanding. Franchise expert Don Daszkowski, the president of Business Mart Inc. and the Franchise Buyers Network, has operated many businesses over the past fifteen years. On the Balance Small Business website, he gives advice to prospective franchise owners:

> In your role as franchisee, you should be prepared to wear many hats. In operating the business, you will most likely have to manage all the daily operations involved in operating a business, including ordering supplies, meeting with customers and vendors, preparing payroll, resolving discrepancies, etc. These are just a few of your "sub-roles" depending on the type of business you are running. It is essential to be able to organize all of your responsibilities so that everything gets done accurately and in a timely manner.

Franchisors will usually provide their franchise owners with a comprehensive manual outlining the company's requirements for all aspects of running the business. This document is often hundreds of pages long, and it is up to the franchise owners to study and thoroughly understand what is in it. They must also be able to communicate the procedures outlined in the manual to all the franchise employees. As with any business, franchise owners are concerned with hiring employees, making sure that they are trained properly for their position, maintaining a safe work environment, and dealing with such problems as poor work habits, attitude problems, and absenteeism.

Franchise owners must also deal with the financial side of the business. This includes working with vendors to make sure that an adequate inventory of supplies and merchandise is always on hand. Some franchise owners are required by contract to purchase supplies exclusively from the franchisor; this allows the company to maintain quality standards throughout its network of franchisees. Other financial considerations include paying ongoing royalty fees to the franchisor and keeping the company advised of the financial position of the franchise owner's operation.

With so much diversity in the franchising world, the responsibilities of one franchise owner may be different from the responsibilities of others. Stuart Field, the owner of a Marco's Pizza franchise in Franklin, Tennessee, arrives at work at about 10:00 a.m. to supervise his employees who are preparing for the lunch rush. He takes walk-in and telephone orders and makes sure the pizzas are ready in ten minutes for the hurried lunchtime customers. After the midday rush, Stuart oversees preparations for the dinner hour. He even does a little marketing on his drive to and from work, introducing himself and passing out menus to prospective customers.

Jeff Stewart owns a Nationwide Floor & Window Coverings franchise. In an interview for the book *Franchise Times: Guide to Selecting, Buying & Owning a Franchise*, Stewart says,

> I call people to set up appointments and present myself directly to the customers or new referral sources. I follow up on initial calls to see if I can warm anything up. I'm also ordering materials, arranging installations, and writing work orders. You have to multitask, and you couldn't do this without cell phones . . . because you have to be available all the time.

These two different types of franchises represent the wide range of business opportunities available to people seeking to become franchise owners. And when a franchise is successful, both the franchisor and the franchisee prosper.

How Do You Become a Franchise Owner?

Education

While a college education can be beneficial in handling the many operations involved in running a franchise, it is not required.

However, high school, community college, or university classes in business, finance, communication, and computer science can provide a franchise owner with essential skills, as will any previous business experience.

The prospective owner must become educated about the industry in which he or she intends to do business, whether it is food service, auto repair, or child care. He or she should also thoroughly research the franchisor, study the local area to determine if a franchise can succeed, and talk to other franchisees to gather inside information about the business. Once a franchise contract is signed, the franchisor will usually provide comprehensive training and ongoing educational support.

Certification and Licensing

Certification is usually not required for purchasing a franchise, but many franchisors have their own certification programs covering various areas of their business. Many fast-food franchises offer the National Restaurant Association Educational Foundation's Food Safety Training and Certification courses to their franchisees. Under the organization's ServSafe program, the online or classroom courses lead to certificates in various aspects of safe food handling. The Institute of Certified Franchise Executives holds continuing education courses leading to the Certified Franchise Executive designation. This certification indicates that franchisees are dedicated to professionalism and maintaining a high standard of quality in their businesses.

Obtaining federal and state business licenses is usually handled by the franchisor, and as of 2017, only fifteen states require licensing. The new franchise owner will be responsible for licenses and permits for building a new facility or remodeling an existing building.

Volunteer Work and Internships

Many franchises offer internships to college students. McDonald's, Starbucks, and other franchisors hire interns, usually for summer employment. With an internship, a student can get firsthand experience in franchise operation, as well as make valuable contacts within the industry.

Skills and Personality

Effective business skills are among the top requirements for a successful franchise owner. Many experts assert that they are more important than a formal education. "Most franchisors," says franchise broker Mike Welch on the AllBusiness website, "are going to give little weight to a person's degree during the selection process. Good franchisors with proven track records are looking for transferable skills that the franchisee can leverage in order to be successful as an owner." These skills include the ability to communicate clearly with employees and customers, a firm grasp of the financial aspects of the business, optimism for the future of the franchise, and the capability to calmly respond when the inevitable setbacks occur.

A franchise owner must be a team player, willing to follow the requirements of the franchisor. Purchasing a franchise means giving up a certain amount of freedom in the way a business is run in exchange for becoming a representative of a well-known brand. If individuality and doing things "my way" is an important job expectation, a person may be better off becoming an entrepreneur and creating an entirely new business rather than signing a franchise agreement.

One of the most common personality traits found in franchise owners is an aversion to taking risks. While there are risks in any business venture, in a franchise operation the franchisors have already taken these risks and determined what works for their business. Good franchisees are comfortable knowing that many of the risks of business ownership have already been addressed.

On the Job

Employers

According to the World Franchise Council, franchise owners are not employees of their franchisor, as is sometimes thought.

Although the franchisor establishes the requirements for its franchise owners, it does not operate as an employer. A franchisee is a business owner who manages the operations of the business and is responsible for hiring, wages, work schedules, and working conditions. By taking on these responsibilities, the franchise owner is the employer.

Working Conditions

Working conditions in the franchise industry vary as widely as the types of franchises. This can range from a typical office setting for financial businesses like Liberty Tax Services to the fast-paced kitchens and dining areas of Burger King and Dairy Queen. Other franchises, such as handyman services, sign shops, and window replacement businesses operate outdoors in all types of weather. These franchises may require the owner to travel to job sites to inspect work progress and instruct crews.

Hard work is perhaps the hallmark of a successful franchise owner. The International Franchising Association reports that managing a franchise is a sixty- to seventy-hour-a-week job, which usually includes evenings and weekends. Some franchisees report that eighty-hour weeks are not uncommon. When starting a new franchise, many owners continue to work at their regular day jobs until the franchise starts bringing in sufficient income. This can cause considerable stress on family life. Eric Stites, the chief executive of the Franchise Business Review, writes in the *Washington Post*, "Franchising is not really an easy path to success. A lot of people are surprised at the amount of effort it takes to get a new business off the ground."

Earnings

As may be expected, franchise owners report a wide range of income, depending on type of franchise, number of franchise units owned, and location. These earnings can be as little as $10,000 to as much as $250,000 or more. According to a survey by Business.com, the median annual franchise income was around $50,000 in 2017. Franchisees who owned three or more units of the same franchise had a median income of $88,000; 16 percent of such owners reported an annual income of more than $250,000.

Opportunities for Advancement

The way most franchise owners advance is by opening additional units of the franchise. When Rob Cookston was nineteen years old, he was delivering Domino's pizzas in his red Volkswagen. Looking for bigger opportunities, he entered the Domino's manager training program. Twenty-five years later, he owned eighteen Domino's franchises. "I worked my way up the Domino's system," Cookston told CNN. "That's the American Dream."

What Is the Future Outlook for Franchise Owners?

Americans love the convenience, reliability, and value of doing business with franchises. This means a healthy future for franchise owners. According to the Franchise Business Economic Outlook study, in 2017 the number of franchise outlets increased by 1.6 percent to 745,290, and employment was up 3.1 percent. The economic output (the value of goods or services produced) of the franchise industry was $713 billion, 5.6 percent higher than the previous year. As these increases are predicted to continue, there will be more opportunities for new franchise owners to become a vital part of the American economy.

Find Out More

American Association of Franchisees and Dealers (AAFD)
PO Box 10158
Palm Desert, CA 92255
website: www.aafd.org

The American Association of Franchisees and Dealers promotes the highest standards in franchising practices for both franchisees and franchisors. The AAFD's Fair Franchising Standards are a guide to judging the quality of a franchise opportunity. The organization offers accreditation of franchisors with its AAFD Fair Franchising Seal.

Blue MauMau
website: www.bluemaumau.org

This website offers the latest news about franchising, tools for franchisees, and numerous resources, including the largest franchise directory on the Internet. Blue MauMau has discussion groups, member blogs, and an online encyclopedia covering all aspects of the franchise industry.

Franchise Times
website: www.franchisetimes.com

This website is the online presence of *Franchise Times* magazine. It offers a wealth of news and information about franchising, including webinars, listings of franchise opportunities, and access to back issues of *Franchise Times*.

International Franchising Association (IFA)
1900 K St. NW, Suite 700
Washington, DC 20006
website: www.franchise.org

The International Franchising Association is the largest organization representing franchising internationally. The IFA promotes franchising through educational programs and government and media relations, and publishes a Statement of Guiding Principles for franchisors and franchisees.

Accountant and Auditor

At a Glance

Accountant and Auditor

Minimum Educational Requirements
Bachelor's degree

Personal Qualities
Mathematical skills; detail oriented; time management and organizational skills; ethical and trustworthy

Certification and Licensing
Certification is required to work with the public

Working Conditions
Office environment; some travel may be required

Salary Range
About $43,020 to $122,200 per year in 2016

Number of Jobs
1,139,700 in 2016

Future Job Outlook
Predicted 10 percent growth through 2026, which is faster than average

What Do Accountants and Auditors Do?

Accountants are responsible for keeping track of an organization's financial operations and performing routine daily financial transactions. This involves maintaining accurate records, such as balance sheets, managing the company's payroll, preparing year-end financial statements, paying vendors, and preparing tax documents. Auditors may sometimes perform similar tasks, but their main responsibility is to verify the accuracy of a company's financial records. The auditor inspects such documents as account books, receipts, vouchers, payroll records, and electronic or paper correspondence to create an unbiased picture of a firm's accounting practices. An auditor may also research a company's history or talk with management to gain a better understanding of the firm's operations and financial reporting methods. A thorough audit may take up to two months to complete.

Accountants are generally employed by a company, but auditors are usually brought in from outside the organization. In contrast to an accountant's daily responsibilities, an auditor might be called in to review a company's books quarterly or annually or at any time that a financial irregularity is suspected. It is often said that the auditor's work begins where the accountant's ends. Both accountants and auditors write reports to management. Accountants suggest ways to improve a company's financial position, and auditors offer opinions about the accuracy of a firm's financial statements.

Accountants may become public accountants and provide their services to companies or individuals as a part of an accounting firm or in their own business. Similarly, auditors may be internal auditors working for a company or external auditors working independently or for auditing firms. Many accountants and auditors specialize. For example, forensic accountants investigate such financial crimes as embezzlement or fraud and prepare evidence for use in court. Auditors may specialize in such areas as health insurance, hospitals and medical facilities, and institutions of higher education.

A twenty-three-year-old staff accountant who works at an accounting firm with seventy-five employees describes her job in the book *Careers in Accounting*:

> I prepare tax returns for individuals, corporations, pension plans, and estates. Our firm is split into four departments: the audit department, which does attest [audit review] work; the bookkeeping department; the information technology consulting department; and the tax department, where I work. We do compliance work and tax returns and deal with other tax-related issues, such as letters from the IRS [Internal Revenue Service].
>
> We have ten partners and umpteen managers with very diverse personalities, and I answer to every one of them. You have to be able to interact with different individuals, so you have to learn for whom you do what and with whom you can and can't joke.

On the website Indeed, Kay, an auditor in Colorado, says, "The good part about being an auditor . . . is that you are constantly learning. Every audit provides new situations and challenges. Legislation and regulations change too, so it seldom gets to be a boring situation."

Jobs in accounting and auditing have historically been characterized by the image of a bookkeeper sitting at a desk, performing monotonous calculations day after day in lonely solitude. While never portrayed as glamorous, accountants and auditors play an important role in maintaining the strength and integrity of the American economy.

How Do You Become an Accountant or Auditor?

Education

The minimum requirement for an accountant or auditor position is a bachelor's degree in accounting or a related field such as business administration. Helpful courses in these disciplines include economics, finance, computer science, management information systems, and international commerce. Larger accounting firms often require an entry-level candidate to have a master's degree in accounting. Although a master's degree in accounting is suitable, many graduate students choose to get a master of business administration (MBA) degree with a concentration in either accounting or finance.

Some colleges and universities offer online courses leading to an undergraduate degree in accounting, as well as courses for acquiring a master's degree. There are also online courses for those who have an undergraduate degree in a field other than accounting or business, which can help in gaining an entry-level accounting position.

Certification and Licensing

The most important certification for accountants is the Certified Public Accountant (CPA) designation. Becoming a CPA allows an accountant to provide such services as financial advising, estate planning, and income tax preparation to the public. Within the private sector, accountants with a CPA designation have greater opportunities for advancement, a higher salary, and the trust and professionalism that comes with obtaining the license.

In most states, a CPA candidate must have a bachelor's degree in accounting, having completed at least 150 credit hours of undergraduate study. The key requirement for obtaining a CPA is passing a rigorous examination. The four-part exam covers auditing, business environment and concepts, financial accounting, and regulation. After completing the exam, one to two years of practical accounting experience is required before a CPA license is issued.

An auditor can become a Certified Internal Auditor (CIA) by following a path similar to the CPA certification. An undergraduate degree from a college or university approved by the Institute of Internal Auditors (IIA), one to two years of work experience, and a passing grade on the CIA exam are required for the CIA certification. The IIA also issues specialized auditing certifications, as do organizations such as the Information Systems Audit and Control Association and the Bank Administration Institute.

Volunteer Work and Internships

Accounting internships are a valuable way to gain practical experience and meet people who may be able to help with career advancement. Many accounting firms, corporations, and independent CPAs offer internships that may provide students with both academic credit and pay. Internships may be offered during the summer or the spring tax season, which is accounting's busiest time of year. Former intern Christina Freeland describes the advantages of an accounting internship on the Accounting Today website:

> After interning I knew that accounting was something I would enjoy for my career because there are many challenges that will keep my career interesting and the goals of accountants are set high, both characteristics that are important to me. I am very happy that I had the opportunity to intern before beginning my career, and I highly recommend an internship for all college students entering the workforce within the next few years.

The IRS provides free income tax advice and preparation services to low-income families and the elderly through its Volunteer Income Tax Assistance and Tax Counseling for the Elderly programs. Volunteering for one of these programs can provide experience for people who plan to become accountants, especially in tax accounting. Volunteers are trained through online or classroom courses in tax return preparation and review. The volunteer work is performed at local community sites, usually at night or on weekends.

Skills and Personality

Accountants and auditors must have good analytical skills to analyze a company's financial history and operational records and provide solutions to help it reach its financial goals. Excellent mathematical skills and accuracy are also vital to accountants and auditors. In addition, they need to have attention to detail, the ability to set priorities and manage time, and strong organizational skills.

Accountants and auditors must also be able to communicate complicated financial concepts in a way that clients can understand. Although accountants have often been characterized as introverted people, having an outgoing personality can be an asset when dealing with the public.

Along with these skills, a successful accountant or auditor must be trustworthy and have a strong commitment to ethical conduct. "Beyond work ethics," says Nicholas Sinclair, the chief executive officer of The Outsourced Accountant, in his company's blog, "a strong sense of integrity is an imperative trait that boosts confidence in an accountant's work. Accountants who live a life of integrity are most likely to obey rules and will ensure to keep confidential information private."

Employers

Most accountants and auditors work in the finance and insurance industries; others work in corporate management, accounting service firms, and the government. The most prestigious accounting and auditing jobs are in the so-called big four accounting/audit firms: Deloitte, PricewaterhouseCoopers, KPMG, and Ernst & Young. Working for one of the big four provides accountants and auditors with a generous salary and benefits, a wide range of experience, a fast track to advancement, and the prestige that comes with working for one of the top international accounting firms.

Accountants and auditors who work for so-called boutique accounting firms generally make less money and, with a boutique's smaller client base, are exposed to a narrower range of experiences. But there is more variety in the type of work assigned, rather than the typical specialization of a job in the big four. There is also less deadline pressure, and more opportunities to gain a close relationship with coworkers.

Working Conditions

While accountants and auditors generally work a forty-hour week, in 2016 about 20 percent of accountants and auditors reported working longer hours. There are also busy periods in which the workload dramatically increases and deadlines quickly approach. These occur throughout tax season (generally from January through April, but also at other times for corporations) and during year-end budget preparation.

Although most of an accountant's and auditor's work is done in an office, travel may be required to visit clients at their places of business. This is especially true in smaller firms, where accountants are more likely to have client contact, and for auditors who must perform their audits on-site.

Earnings

The Bureau of Labor Statistics (BLS) reports that the median salary for accountants and auditors in 2016 was $68,150. Annual wages ranged from $43,020 for the lowest 10 percent to $122,200 for the highest 10 percent.

Opportunities for Advancement

In most accounting firms, the first few years are a training period for new accountants and auditors. After gaining experience, a junior accountant or auditor may advance to a senior accounting or auditing position or move into management. Accountants with a CPA designation may choose to open their own independent public accounting firms. In the big four firms, the path to advancement is structured. A bright junior staff accountant can regularly move up the corporate ladder, aiming for the ultimate goal of becoming a senior partner with a salary and bonuses that can reach $1 million or more. Auditors in these firms may, after years of experience, specialize in industry, managing the audits of multibillion-dollar corporations.

What Is the Future Outlook for Accountants and Auditors?

According to the BLS, the job outlook for accountants and auditors is projected to grow 10 percent through 2026. This is faster than the growth rate for all industries. The strength of the economy will have an impact on this growth rate: if the economy continues to expand, more accountants and auditors will be needed. Other factors that can affect the job market include the continued expansion of globalization, future changes in tax legislation, increased vigilance against corporate fraud, and technological advances that may automate some lower-level jobs.

Find Out More

Accounting Degree Review
website: www.accounting-degree.org

This website offers comprehensive information about education for prospective accountants and auditors. It includes rankings of college accounting programs, informative articles about the accounting and auditing industry, and blogs about internships, degree programs, and finding a job.

American Institute of Certified Professional Accountants (AICPA)
220 Leigh Farm Rd.
Durham, NC 27707
website: www.aicpa.org

The American Institute of Certified Professional Accountants is the world's largest organization for the accounting profession, with more than four hundred thousand members. The AICPA sets ethical and auditing standards for the profession. Its website provides resources and practical information for young or aspiring accountants.

Institute of Internal Auditors
1035 Greenwood Blvd., Suite 401
Lake Mary, FL 32746
website: https://na.theiia.org

The Institute of Internal Auditors in North America is the official voice of the internal auditing profession, providing resources and certification for internal auditors. It provides information for students seeking information about auditing careers, including tips for job seekers, a career guide, and a wide range of grants, scholarships, and awards.

Professional Accounting Society of America (PASA)
300-1331 Macleod Trail SE
Calgary, AB T2G 0K3
Canada
website: www.thepasa.org

The PASA is the professional organization for entry- and midlevel accountants working at accounting firms across America. The College Corner section of its website contains a wealth of information for students considering accounting as a career, including access to informative articles, scholarship opportunities, and local membership events.

Interview with a Public Relations Specialist

Megan Godfrey is the group account director at KemperLesnik, a public relations, marketing, and communications company headquartered in Chicago. The company specializes in public relations (PR) as well as event, content, and sports marketing. This last area is a perfect fit for Godfrey, who was a professional golfer before joining the firm. Among her duties at KemperLesnik have been leading communication efforts for a portfolio of luxury golf destinations and major golf championships. She discussed her career with the author via e-mail.

Q: Why did you become a public relations specialist?
A: My path to PR was unconventional. After playing professional golf, I was offered a job with a start-up company in Chicago. I was tasked with managing the company's PR agency. And, it was a learning process. I quickly saw that writing was an important part of the job and that I could excel in this field. Later, I became responsible for media and blogger relations, where I learned how to perfect a pitch and persuade journalists to write about our company's products. Reading the stories that I helped to secure was the most satisfying part of the job. I was also encouraged to learn the business from great leaders and mentors throughout my career.

Q: Can you describe your typical workday?
A: No, because no two days are the same! This can be both exciting and frustrating. Technology keeps our team connected at

all times and allows us to work from any location in the world—from the office, to a media center at a golf course, to a client site, to a TV station, and everywhere in between!

Q: What do you like most about your job?
A: I enjoy the variety, the fast-paced nature of the job, and the wide range of projects and clients that our agency manages. We have a very collaborative, energetic team, which fosters creativity, and we're fortunate to work with great clients who represent exceptional brands.

Q: What do you like least about your job?
A: Working in sports PR can be exhausting. During the busiest times of the year, my job requires long hours and work during weekends and holidays. The administrative responsibilities, such as time tracking and reporting, can also be tiring.

Q: What personal qualities do you find most valuable for this type of work?
A: In an agency, the best PR professionals are those who take initiative and can manage multiple projects at one time. We also expect our team to be detail oriented and organized because it improves productivity and makes multitasking easier. Finally, to excel in a PR agency, it's crucial for our staff to be flexible and open to change—both with project deadlines and client work. Agency business frequently changes from year to year based on new clients, new project assignments, or notable events. It's important to be flexible to this change and seize new opportunities to learn a new industry or expand your skill set.

Q: What is the best way to prepare for this type of job?
A: The single best way to prepare for a job in PR is to hone your writing skills and become a ruthless editor of your own written communications. Writing is an essential part of the job at every level of the industry. I would also recommend that new graduates read about the PR industry and stay updated with current

events and daily news. Finally, if you want to work in an agency, I would read about the agency's background and the clients that the agency represents.

Q: What other advice do you have for students who might be interested in this career?

A: Networking is an important tool throughout your career. Build a network of colleagues, friends, and mentors and continue to maintain it as you grow. I would also encourage students to be relentless, but polite, in their follow-up and job pursuit. I always remember the few people who follow up with me immediately after a brief meeting or interview. It tells me that they are committed and reliable—both good qualities for a new hire. Finally, practice your communication skills, both written and verbal communications. It's vital for success in any career, but especially in public relations.

Other Jobs in Business

- Accounts payable/receivable specialist
- Actuary
- Advertising copywriter
- Assessor
- Bookkeeper
- Budget analyst
- Cashier
- Cost estimator
- Credit manager
- Customer service representative
- Database manager
- Event coordinator
- Executive assistant
- Food service manager
- Fund-raiser
- Hotel front desk associate
- Human resources specialist
- Insurance underwriter
- Inventory associate
- Labor relations specialist
- Loan officer
- Loss-prevention specialist
- Media buyer
- Media director
- Merchandise buyer
- Office manager
- Real estate agent
- Sales clerk
- Software designer
- Stockbroker
- Store manager/assistant manager
- Travel agent
- Warehouse manager
- Website designer

Editor's Note: The US Department of Labor's Bureau of Labor Statistics provides information about hundreds of occupations. The agency's *Occupational Outlook Handbook* describes what these jobs entail, the work environment, education and skill requirements, pay, future outlook, and more. The *Occupational Outlook Handbook* may be accessed online at www.bls.gov/ooh.

Index

Note: Boldface page numbers indicate illustrations.

Abell, Mark, 32
Access Perks (website), 20
accountants and auditors
    advancement opportunities, 72
    basic facts about, 66
    business profitability and, 4
    certification and licensing, 68–69
    earnings, **6**, 71
    educational requirements, **6**, 68
    employers, 67, 70–71
    information sources, 72–73
    job description, 66–68, 71
    job outlook, 72
    personal qualities and skills, 70
    volunteer work and internships, 69–70
Accounting Degree Review (website), 72
Accounting Today (website), 69
Accredited in Public Relations (APR) credential, 45, 48
Advertising Research Foundation (ARF), 15
advertising specialists, 4
    See also public relations specialists
AllBusiness (website), 62
American Association of Franchisees and Dealers (AAFD), 64–65
American Association of Public Opinion Research (AAPOR), 15–16
American Finance Association (AFA), 40–41
American Institute of Certified Professional Accountants (AICPA), 73
American Management Association (AMA), 24, 41
American Marketing Association (AMA), 11, 16
Association for Financial Professionals (AFP), 37, 41
Association for Talent Development (ATD), 21, 25
auditing clerks, **6**
auditors. *See* accountants and auditors

Balance Careers (website), 19
Balance Small Business (website), 59
Bank Administration Institute, 69
benefits. *See* earnings
Bereketli, Ezgi, 35
big four accounting/audit firms, 71
Blue MauMau (website), 65
bookkeepers, **6**
B2B International (website), 10
Bureau of Labor Statistics (BLS)
    earnings
        accountants and auditors, 71
        financial analysts, 39–40
        market research analysts, 14
        public relations specialists, 47–48
        sales engineers, 55
        training and development specialists, 23
    educational requirements for sales engineers, 53
    employers
        market research analysts, 13
        sales engineers, 54
        training and development specialists, 23
    job outlooks
        accountants and auditors, 72
        business jobs predicted to decline, 7
        financial analysts, 40
        market research analysts, 15
        public relations specialists, 48
        sales engineers, 56
        training and development specialists, 24
    Occupational Outlook Handbook, 77
    working hours of sales engineers, 55
business
    career opportunities in, 4, 77
    defining, 4
    types of, 4
Business.com, 63–64
Business Insider (website), 7

Care, John, 56
Careers in Accounting, 67
cashiers, **6**
certification and licensing
    accountants and auditors, 66, 68–69
    financial analysts, 34, 37
    franchise owners, 58, 61
    market research analysts, 8, 11
    public relations specialists, 42, 45
    sales engineers, 50, 53, 57
    small business owners, 26, 29
    training and development specialists, 17, 21
Certified Franchise Executive designation, 61
Certified Internal Auditor (CIA) certification, 69
Certified Manufacturing Technology Sales Engineer credential, 53
Certified Professional in Learning and Performance certificates, 21
Certified Professional Manufacturers Representative, 57
Certified Professional Sales Person credential, 53
Certified Public Accountant (CPA) designation, 68–69, 72
Certified Training and Development Professional certificates, 21
CFA Institute, 37, 41
chartered financial analyst (CFA) credential, 37
Cisco (blog), 52
Cision (website), 44
CityTownInfo (website), 39
Cookston, Rob, 64
customer service representatives, **6**

Dalrymple, Alyssa, 11–12
Daszkowski, Don, 59
Deloitte, 71
Digest of Education Statistics (National Center for Education Statistics), 5
Donnelly, Ted, 9

earnings, **6**
    accountants and auditors, **6**, 66, 71

financial analysts, 34, 39–40
franchise owners, 58, 63–64
market research analysts, **6**, 8, 14
public relations specialists, 42, 47–48
sales engineers, 50, 55–56
small business owners, 26, 32
training and development specialists, 17, 23
educational requirements, 5–7, **6**
   accountants and auditors, **6**, 66, 68
   financial analysts, 34, 36
   franchise owners, 58, 60–61
   market research analysts, **6**, 8, 10–11
   public relations specialists, 42, 44–45
   sales engineers, 50, 52–53
   small business owners, 26, 28–29
   training and development specialists, 17, 20–21
Edwards, Akin, 51, 52
employers
   accountants and auditors, 67, 70–71
   financial analysts, 38–39
   franchise owners and, 62–63
   market research analysts, 13–14
   public relations specialists, 47
   sales engineers, 54
   small businesses and, 26, 31
   training and development specialists, 23
Ernst & Young, 71

Field, Stuart, 60
field marketers, 9
financial analysts
   advancement opportunities, 40
   basic facts about, 34
   business profitability and, 4
   certification and licensing, 37
   earnings, 39–40
   educational requirements, 36
   employers, 38–39
   information sources, 40–41
   job description, 34–36, 39
   job outlook, 40
   personal qualities and skills, 38
   volunteer work and internships, 37–38
Financial Industry Regulatory Authority (FINRA), 37
FlexMR (website), 13
Food Safety Training and Certification courses (National Restaurant Association Educational Foundation), 61
food service managers, **6**
Forbes (website), 27, 35
Fortune Marketing Company (website), 30
Franchise Business Economic Outlook, 64
franchise owners (franchisees)
   advancement opportunities, 64
   basic facts about, 58
   certification and licensing, 61
   earnings, 63–64
   educational requirements, 60–61
   employers and, 62–63
   information sources, 64–65
   job description, 58–60, 63
   job outlook, 64
   personal qualities and skills, 62
   volunteer work and internships, 61–62
Franchise Times (website), 65
Franchise Times: Guide to Selecting, Buying & Owning a Franchise, 60
Freeland, Christina, 69

Getting There from Here: Career Path Stories from Finance Professionals (Kaplan University), 34, 36
G.I. Jobs (website), 22

Godfrey, Megan, 74–76
Goldman Sachs (website), 37–38

Harmon, Drew, 36
Harrison, Matthew, 10
Hart, Sandee, 43–44
Heathfield, Susan, 19
Hess, Lisa, 43
Higgins, Carolyn, 30
Howell, Amy, 44
human resources specialists, **6**

Indeed (website), 68
Information Systems Audit and Control Association, 69
Insights Association, 11, 16
Institute for Performance and Learning, 21
Institute of Certified Franchise Executives, 61
Institute of Internal Auditors (IIA), 69, 73
insurance underwriters, **6**
International Association of Business Communicators (IABC), 48–49
International Franchising Association (IFA), 63, 65
International Society for Performance Improvement (ISPI), 25
IRS programs, 70

job descriptions
   accountants and auditors, 66–68, 71
   advertising specialists, 4
   financial analysts, 34–36, 39
   franchise owners, 58–60, 63
   managers, 4
   market research analysts, 4, 8–10, **12**, 14
   public relations specialists, 42–44, 47, 74–75
   sales engineers, 50–52, 55
   sales executives, 4
   small business owners, 26–28, **30**, 31
   training and development specialists, 4, 17–20, **19**, 23
job outlooks
   accountants and auditors, 66, 72
   best business jobs, 7
   business jobs predicted to decline, 7
   financial analysts, 34, 40
   franchise owners, 58, 64
   market research analysts, 8, 15
   number of jobs created by small businesses, 26
   public relations specialists, 42, 48
   sales engineers, 50, 56
   small business owners, 26, 32
   training and development specialists, 17, 24
Johnson, Holly, 31

Kaiden, Sue, 22
Kaplan University, 34, 36
Kappel, Mike, 27
Karthik, Akshay, 53–54
KPMG, 71

Lainas, Greg, 38
licensing. *See* certification and licensing
loan officers, **6**

managers, 4
Manufacturers' Agents National Association (MANA), 56–57
Manufacturers' Representatives Educational Research Foundation, 57
market research analysts
   advancement opportunities, 14–15
   basic facts about, 8
   certification and licensing, 11
   earnings, **6**, 14
   educational requirements, **6**, 10–11

employers, 13–14
information sources, 15–16
job description, 4, 8–10, **12**, 14
job outlook, 15
personal qualities and skills, 12–13
specialties, 9
volunteer work and internships, 11–12
Medium (website), 53–54
meSE, 53

National Association of Sales Professionals (NASP), 53, 57
National Center for Education Statistics, 5
National Communication Association (NCA), 49
National Restaurant Association Educational Foundation, 61

Okta (website), 51
Outsourced Accountant, The (blog), 70
OwlGuru (website), 12–13

PayScale (website), 32
personal qualities and skills
    accountants and auditors, 66, 70
    financial analysts, 34, 38
    franchise owners, 58, 62
    market research analysts, 8, 12–13
    public relations specialists, 42, 46–47, 75
    sales engineers, 50, 54
    small business owners, 26, 29–30
    training and development specialists, 17, 21–22
PR Daily (website), 47
Presti, Ken, 52
PricewaterhouseCoopers, 71
Professional Accounting Society of America (PASA), 73
professional researcher certificates (PRCs), 11
Public Relations Society of America (PRSA), 45, 49
public relations specialists
    advancement opportunities, 48
    basic facts about, 42
    certification and licensing, 45
    earnings, 47–48
    educational requirements, 44–45
    employers, 47
    information sources, 48–49
    job description, 42–44, 47, 74–75
    job outlook, 48
    personal qualities and skills, 46–47, 75
    volunteer work and internships, 45–46
Public Relations Student Society of America (PRSSA), 49

Quinlan, Chelsea, 45–46

Raanes, Brady, 34–35
real estate brokers and sales agents, **6**
Robles, Lisa, 22

"Sales Engineer Career Path, The" (Care), 56
Sales Engineer Certification, 53
sales engineers
    advancement opportunities, 56
    basic facts about, 50
    certification and licensing, 53, 57
    earnings, 55–56
    educational requirements, 52–53
    employers, 54
    information sources, 56–57
    job description, 50–52, 55
    job outlook, 56
    personal qualities and skills, 54
    volunteer work and internships, 53–54

sales executives, 4
SCORE (Service Corps of Retired Executives), 29, 33
ServSafe program (National Restaurant Association Educational Foundation), 61
Sinclair, Nicholas, 70
Small Business Administration (SBA)
    definition of small business, 26
    information about, 33
    programs for development of skills of small business owners, 28–29
small business owners
    advancement opportunities, 32
    basic facts about, 26
    certification and licensing, 29
    earnings, 32
    educational requirements, 28–29
    information sources, 33
    job description, 26–28, **30**, 31
    job outlook, 32
    personal qualities and skills, 29–30
    self-employment and, 31
    volunteer work and internships, 29
Small Business Pulse Survey, 31
SmartBear, 52
SmartBiz (website), 33
Society for Human Resource Management (SHRM), 25
software developers, **6**
Stewart, Jeff, 60
Stites, Eric, 63

Tax Counseling for the Elderly (IRS program), 70
telemarketers, 9
TheSelfEmployed.com (website), 33
Top Sales World (website), 57
TopUniversities.com, 5
training and development specialists
    advancement opportunities, 23–24
    basic facts about, 17
    certification and licensing, 21
    earnings, 24
    educational requirements, 20–21
    employers, 23
    information sources, 24–25
    job description, 4, 17–20, **19**, 23
    job outlook, 24
    personal qualities and skills, 21–22
    volunteer work and internships, 21
travel agents, **6**
Tucker, Laura, 5–7

U.S. News & World Report (magazine), 9

Virtual Inc. (website), 18
Volunteer Income Tax Assistance (IRS program), 70
volunteer work and internships
    accountants and auditors, 69–70
    financial analysts, 37–38
    franchise owners, 61–62
    market research analysts, 11–12
    public relations specialists, 45–46
    sales engineers, 53–54
    small business owners, 29
    training and development specialists, 21

Washington Post (newspaper), 63
Welch, Mike, 62
WiseBread (website), 31
World Franchise Council, 62–63
Wynans, Kim, 18